Isabel Jones and Curabel Lee rub shoulders with Mingram Mo and a host of familiar creatures from the garden and beyond in this marvellous introduction to the fun and excitement of poetry. David McCord is a much anthologized poet, and this well-known collection includes many of his best loved works for younger children. Here are poems you will long to learn by heart, and many you will want to read and re-read. His dexterity with words and his sparkling humour provide a constant source of surprise and entertainment.

David McCord, born in 1897, is an American academican who has written many books in the fields of education, art, medicine and history. However, he is best known for the freshness and vitality of his verse for children, and *Mr Bidery's Spidery Garden*, his first collection to be published outside America, and now available for the first time in paperback, has become a modern classic.

Mr Bidery's Spidery Garden

Poems by David McCord

Illustrated by Penny Dann

PUFFIN BOOKS

PUFFIN BOOKS

Published by the Penguin Group
27 Wrights Lane, London W8 5TZ, England
Viking Penguin Inc., 40 West 23rd Street, New York, New York 10010, USA
Penguin Books Australia Ltd, Ringwood, Victoria, Australia
Penguin Books Canada Ltd, 2801 John Street, Markham, Ontario, Canada L3R 1B4
Penguin Books (NZ) Ltd, 182–190 Wairau Road, Auckland 10, New Zealand

Penguin Books Ltd, Registered Offices: Harmondsworth, Middlesex, England

First published in Great Britain by George G. Harrap & Co. Ltd 1972
Published in Puffin Books 1989
1 3 5 7 9 10 8 6 4 2

This edition copyright © David McCord, 1972
Illustrations copyright © Penny Dann, 1989
All rights reserved

Made and printed in Great Britain by Cox & Wyman Ltd, Reading

To my English cousin
Charlotte Sara Rentoul
even before she can read

Blesséd Lord, what it is to be young:
To be of, to be for, be among —
  Be enchanted, enthralled,
  Be the caller, the called,
The singer, the song, and the sung.

Father and I in the Woods

"Son,"
My father used to say,
"Don't run."

"Walk,"
My father used to say,
"Don't talk."

"Words,"
My father used to say,
"Scare birds."

So be:
It's sky and brook and bird
And tree.

Contents

Mr Bidery's Spidery Garden

Poor old Mr Bidery.
His garden's awfully spidery:
Bugs use it as a hidery.

In April it was secdery,
By May a mess of weedery;
And oh, the bugs! How greedery.

White flowers out or buddery,
Potatoes made it spuddery;
And when it rained, what muddery!

June days grow long and shaddery;
Bullfrog forgets his taddery;
The spider legs his laddery.

With cabbages so odory,
Snapdragon soon explodery,
At twilight all is toadary.

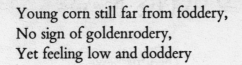

Young corn still far from foddery,
No sign of goldenrodery,
Yet feeling low and doddery

Is poor old Mr Bidery,
His garden lush and spidery,
His apples green, not cidery.

Pea-picking *is* so poddery!

The Newt

The little newt
Is not a brute,
A fish or fowl,
A kind of owl:
He doesn't prowl
Or run or dig
Or grow too big.
He doesn't fly
Or laugh or cry —
He doesn't try.

The little newt
Is mostly mute,
And grave and wise,
And has two eyes.
He lives inside,
Or likes to hide;
But after rain
He's out again
And rather red,
I should have said.

The little newt
Of great repute
Has legs, a tail,
A spotted veil.
He walks alone
From stone to stone,
From log to log,
From bog to bog,
From tree to tree,
From you to me.

The little newt
By grass or root
Is very kind
But hard to find.
His hands and feet
Are always neat:
They move across
The mildest moss.
He's very shy,
He's never spry —
Don't ask me why.

The Grasshopper

Down
a
deep
well
a
grasshopper
fell.

By kicking about
He thought to get out.
    He might have known better,
    For that got him wetter.
To kick round and round
Is the way to get drowned,
    And drowning is what
    I should tell you he got.

But
the
well
had
a
rope
that
dangled
some
hope.

And sure as molasses
On one of his passes
    He found the rope handy
    And up he went, *and he*

it
up
and
it
up
and
it
up
and
it
up
went

And hopped away proper
As any grasshopper.

Snail

This sticky trail
Was made by snail.
Snail makes no track
That he'll take back.
However slow,
His word is go.
(Twixt me and you
The word is goo.)

The Starfish

When I see a starfish
Upon the shining sand,
I ask him how he liked the sea
And if he likes the land.
"Would you rather be a starfish
Or an out-beyond-the-bar fish?"
I whisper very softly,
And he seems to understand.

He never *says* directly,
But I fancy all the same
That he knows the answer quite as well
As if it were his name:
"An out-beyond-the-bar fish
Is much happier than a starfish";
And when I look for him again
He's gone the way he came.

Up from Down Under

The boomerang and kangaroo
comprise a very pleasant two;
The coolibah and billabong
together make a sort of song.
But tasty as a fresh meringue
is billabong with boomerang;
and better than hooray-hoorah
is kangaroo with coolibah.

Joe

We feed the birds in winter,
And outside in the snow
We have a tray of many seeds
For many birds of many breeds
And one grey squirrel named Joe.
    But Joe comes early,
    Joe comes late,
    And all the birds
    Must stand and wait.
And waiting there for Joe to go
Is pretty cold work in the snow.

Waltzing Mice

Every night as I go to bed
I think of the prayer I should have said;
And even now as I bow my head:
"Please, O Lord, may I have instead
Some waltzing mice, a gun, and a sled?"

I don't suppose they're much of a price,
But Uncle Ted (without advice)
Gave me skates, and there isn't ice;
And I could have been saying, "How terribly *nice*,
A gun, a sled, and waltzing mice!"

Every night when play is done,
I think them all over, one by one;
"And quite the splendidest, Lord, for fun
Are waltzing mice, a sled, and a gun."

Owls Talking

I think that many owls say *Who-o*:
At least the owls that I know do-o.
But somewhere when some owls do not-t,
Perhaps they cry *Which-h*, *Why-y*, or *What-t*.

    Or when they itch-h
    They just say *Which-h*,
    Or close one eye-e
    And try *What-t Why-y*.

Our Mr Toad

Our Mr Toad
Has a nice abode
Under the first front step.
When it rains he's cool
In a secret pool
Where the water goes
    drip
    drop
    drep.

Our Mr Toad
Will avoid the road:
He's a private–cellar man.
And it's not much fun
In the broiling sun
When you *have* a good
    ten
    tone
    tan.

Our Mr Toad
Has a kind of code
That tells him the coast is clear.
Then away he'll hop
With a stop, stop, stop
When the dusk draws
    nigh
    no
    near.

Crows

I like to walk
And hear the black crows talk.

I like to lie
And watch crows sail the sky.

I like the crow
That wants the wind to blow:

I like the one
That thinks the wind is fun.

I like to see
Crows spilling from a tree,

And try to find
The top crow left behind.

I like to hear
Crows caw that spring is near.

I like the great
Wild clamour of crow hate

Three farms away
When owls are out by day.

I like the slow
Tired homeward-flying crow;

I like the sight
Of crows for my good night.

Little

Little wind, little sun,
Little tree — only one.
Little bird, little wing,
Little song he can sing.
Little need he should stay,
Little *up*-now, away
Little speck, and he's far
Where all little things are.
Little things for me too:
Little sad that he flew.

Conversation

"Mother, may I stay up tonight?"
"No, dear."
"Oh dear! (She always says 'No, dear').
But Father said I might."
"No, dear."
"He did, that is, if you thought it right."
"No, dear, it isn't right."
"Oh dear! Can I keep on the light?"
"No, dear. In spite
Of what your Father said,
You go to bed,
And in the morning you'll be bright
And glad instead
For one more day ahead."
"I might,
But not for one more night."
"No, dear — *no*, dear."
"At least I've been polite, I guess."
"Yes, dear, you've been polite —
Good night."
"Oh dear,
I'd rather stay down here —
I'm quite . . ."
"No, dear. Now, out of sight."
("Well that was pretty near —")
"*Good* night."
("— all right.")
"Good *night*!"

Daybreak

Dawn? blinks Fawn.
What's going on?

Day! screams Jay:
Day, *Day* — Today!

That's so, caws Crow.
You didn't know?

Faint streak of light:
Check that, Bob White?

We see it: Squa-a-a-w-w-k!
(three Nighthawks talk).

Too loud, cries Cloud:
You boys too loud!

You want to wake
some sleepy Snake?

Or hear me sing?
chirps Chipperwing.

Amen to *that!*
squeaks Flit the Bat.

Amen to flittern,
too, booms Bittern.

I cease to prowl
at dawn, says Owl;

You mean you perch
on *me*, brags Birch.

In truth, in troth,
murmurmurs Moth

who likes it dark
in Birch's bark.

Sky's *really* grey
now. *Day!* screams Jay.

Yes. Take a look,
says Trout in Brook.

You see that Fly?
Well, so do I.

I'll leave this ring
where Swallows wing.

Day's night for Fox;
to heck with clocks!

All's night for Moles
like us in holes.

Me too! I surface,
though, says Shrew.

Get off my ground!
cracks Scamperound,

the Squirrel. *My* log!
pipes Lep, the Frog.

Crawl under, Bug,
with me — with Slug.

OK, says Tree:
not under me.

Not under *him?*
mocks Broken Limb,

that tough old Oak?
I'm glad I broke.

You used to toss
in wind, says Moss;

you're rotten wood
now — very good.

Don't leave *your* house,
I notice, Mouse!

He's scared of Cat,
whines Water Rat.

Who wouldn't be?
twits Phoebe. We

birds have a slew
of danger. You

folks hide at will;
we fly, sit still.

A lot of harm
there, round that farm;

not Cow, of course,
or Pig, or Horse;

but Cat and Shrike
and Hawk — suchlike.

The woods are best:
here's where we nest.

Peek in, now. *Hush!*
says Hermit Thrush.

No nest of mine,
pants Porcupine:

all woods are tough.
I've had enough.

Old noisy Quill:
Keep still! Keep still!

You! Silence now!
That Farmer's Cow?

Just sound of axe,
quacks Duck. Relax.

Drum . . . *Drum?* Just some
old Grouse's drum.

No! *No!* thumps Snow-
shoe Rabbit. *No!*

That's Silver Tongue:
Hot Dog! He's young.

But on the loose,
warns Wren. Vamoose!

Run, run! bangs Gun,
lest you be done.

Where? *Where?* grunts Bear,
who looks like Scare.

Here, answers Deer,
who leaps like Fear . . .

No, *no!* says Doe.
It can't be so . . .

on, on, with Fawn.
Why *must* it dawn?

Think! Think! No, slink
away like Mink.

Hide! Hide! some Groundhog
whistles. *Hide!*

O bunk! sniffs Skunk,
the one with spunk.

Isabel Jones & Curabel Lee

Isabel Jones & Curabel Lee
Lived on butter and bread and tea,
And as to that they would both agree:
Isabel, Curabel, Jones & Lee.

Isabel said: While prunes have stones
They aren't a promising food for Jones;
Curabel said: Well, as for me,
Tripe is a terrible thing for Lee.

There's not a dish of fowl or fish
For which we wish, said I. & C.
And that is why until we die
We'll eat no pie, nor beg nor buy
But butter and bread and a trace of tea.
(Signed) *Isabel Jones & Curabel Lee.*

Fast and Slow

The Snail is slow. The swift Gazelle
Could never manage with a shell.

The Snail, without his shell, would squirm
And look a lot like half a worm.

To find him, you would need to peek
Inside some nasty robin's beak.

The poor Gazelle must run to stay
Alive. And that's about the way

It is with Snails and swift Gazelles:
Some have, and some do not have, shells.

Two Chants

I

Every time I climb a tree
Every time I climb a tree
Every time I climb a tree
I scrape a leg
Or skin a knee
And every time I climb a tree
I find some ants
Or dodge a bee
And get the ants
All over me

And every time I climb a tree
Where have you been?
They say to me
But don't they know that I am free
Every time I climb a tree?
I like it best
To spot a nest
That has an egg
Or maybe three

And then I skin
The other leg
But every time I climb a tree
I see a lot of things to see
Swallows rooftops and TV
And all the fields and farms there be
Every time I climb a tree
Though climbing may be good for ants
It isn't awfully good for pants
But still it's pretty good for me
Every time I climb a tree

II

The pickety fence
The pickety fence
Give it a lick it's
The pickety fence
Give it a lick it's
A clickety fence
Give it a lick it's
A lickety fence
Give it a lick
Give it a lick
Give it a lick
With a rickety stick
Pickety
Pickety
Pickety
Pick.

Snowflakes

Sometime this winter if you go
To walk in soft new-falling snow
When flakes are big and come down slow

To settle on your sleeve as bright
As stars that couldn't wait for night,
You won't know what you have in sight —

Another world — unless you bring
A magnifying glass. This thing
We call a snowflake is the king

Of crystals. Do you like surprise?
Examine him three times his size:
At first you won't believe your eyes.

Stars look alike, but flakes do not:
No two the same in all the lot
That you will get in any spot

You chance to be, for every one
Come spinning through the sky has none
But his own window-wings of sun:

Joints, points, and crosses. What could make
Such lacework with no crack or break?
In billion billions, no mistake?

Take Sky

Now think of words. Take *sky*
And ask yourself just why —
Like sun, moon, star, and cloud —
It sounds so well out loud,
And pleases so the sight
When printed black on white.
Take syllable and thimble:
The sound of *them* is nimble.
Take bucket, spring, and dip
Cold water to your lip.
Take balsam, fir, and pine:
Your woodland smell and mine.
Take kindle, blaze, and flicker —
What lights the hearth fire quicker?

Three words we fear but form:
Gale, twister, thunderstorm;
Others that simply shake
Are tremble, temblor, quake.
But granite, stone, and rock:
Too solid, they, to shock.
Put honey, bee, and flower
With sunny, shade, and shower;
Put *wild* with bird and wing,
Put *bird* with song and sing.
Aren't paddle, trail, and camp
The cabin and the lamp?
Now look at words of rest —
Sleep, quiet, calm, and blest;

At words we learn in youth —
Grace, skill, ambition, truth;
At words of lifelong need —
Grit, courage, strength, and deed;
Deep-rooted words that say
Love, hope, dream, yearn, and pray;
Light-hearted words — girl, boy,
Live, laugh, play, share, enjoy.
October, April, June —
Come late and gone too soon.
Remember, words are life:
Child, husband, mother, wife;
Remember, and I'm done:
Words taken one by one

Are poems as they stand —
Shore, beacon, harbour, land;
Brook, river, mountain, vale,
Crow, rabbit, otter, quail;
Faith, freedom, water, snow,
Wind, weather, flood, and floe.
Like light across the lawn
Are morning, sea, and dawn;
Words of the green earth growing —
Seed, soil, and farmer sowing.
Like wind upon the mouth
Sad, summer, rain, and south.
Amen. Put not asunder
Man's *first* word: wonder . . . wonder . . .

Kite

I flew my kite
One bright blue day,
Light yellow-orangey away
Above the tip tall tops of trees,
With little drops from breeze to breeze,
With little rises and surprises,
And the string would sing to these.

I flew my kite
One white new day,
Bright orange-yellowy and gay
Against the clouds. I flew it through
The cloudiness of one or two —
Careering, veering, disappearing;
String to fingers, tight and true.

I flew my kite
One dole-dark day,
Dull orange image in the grey,
When not a single bird would fly
So windy wet and wild a sky
Of little languors and great angers.
Kite, *good-bye, good-bye, good-bye!*

49

Scat ! Scitten !

Even though
a cat has a kitten,
not a rat has a ritten,
not a bat has a bitten,
not a gnat has a gnitten,
not a sprat has a spritten.
That is that — that is thitten.

Where ?

Where is that little pond I wish for?
Where are those little fish to fish for?

Where is my little rod for catching?
Where are the bites that I'll be scratching?

Where is my rusty reel for reeling?
Where is my trusty creel for creeling?

Where is the line for which I'm looking?
Where are those handy hooks for hooking?

Where is the worm I'll have to dig for?
Where are the boots that I'm too big for?

Where is there *any* boat for rowing?
Where is . . . ?

     Well, anyway, it's snowing.

Alphabet
(Eta Z)

1

A is one
And we've begun.

2

B is two —
Myself and you.

3

C is three —
You, who? and me.

4

D is four;
Let's close the door.

5

E is five
Bees in a hive.

6

F is six
Fat candlesticks.

7

G is seven
And not eleven.

8

H is eight,
And gaining weight.

9

I is nine,
Of slender spine;

10

J is ten.
And then what? Then

11

Comes K eleven
Which isn't seven.

1 2

L is twelve,
Or two-thirds elve.

1 3

M thirteen
Stands in between

1 4

Your A, my Z.
N's fourteen. We

1 5

Now come to O;
Fifteen or so —

1 6

Fifteen, I guess;
P Sixteen. Yes,

1 7

Since seventeen
Cries Q for Queen!

18

Eighteen is R,
The end of star;

19

Nineteen is S
As in success;

20

T's twenty, twice
What ten was; nice

21

To add one to
And capture U,

22

Or add a pair
That V can share.

23

Your twenty-three's
In wow! Xerxes

24

Shows X the core
Of twenty-four.

25

Y keeps alive
In twenty-five;

26

Z's in a fix:
Poor twenty-six!

Frog Music

In a boggy old bog
by a loggy old log
sat a froggy old frog.

He had spots on his skin;
on his face was a grin
that was wide and was thin.

He was green. He was fat
as an old Cheshire cat.
He was flat where he sat.

While he hoped that a fly
would fly by by-and-by,

it was also his wish
to avoid Mr. Fish,

Mr. Turtle, and tall
Mr. Heron, since all
of them *might* pay a call,

and just *might* be aware
of his grin, skin, and bare

bulgy head and those eyes,
very goggly in size.

So he grinned and just sat,
sat and sat, sat and sat,
looking silly like that.

But no fish saw him grin,
thinking, *Now* he'll jump in!

and no turtle a–cruise
thought him there in the ooze,

as a heron on one
leggy leg would have done.
Not a twitch in him — none.

Isn't life pretty grim
for a frog? Think of him.

But then think of that fly
flying by by-and-by.

LMNTL

"Albert, have you a turtle?"
I'll say to him, and Bert'll
say "Yes! Of *course* I have a turtle."

But if I write,
"Have you a trtl, Albert?"
(as I might)
I wonder if Brtl guess
just what I mean?

We all have seen
a dog's tail wagl,
haven't we?
We all agree
that what a dogldo,
a polywogl too.

We've hrd a brd, grls gigl;
observed how skwrls hnt
for nuts; how big pigs grnt;
know how we feel
on hearing young pigsqweel.

Bbbbs buzz, and ktns play;
bats flitrfly azootowls cry.

Why don't we *spell* that way?
Make ibx look like gnu?
Lfnts too; zbras inizoo?
I do. Do you?

Summer Shower

Window window window pane:
Let it let it let it rain
Drop by drop by drop by drop.

Run your rivers from the top
Zigzaggy down, like slow wet forks
Of lightning, so the slippery corks
Of bubbles float and overtake
Each other 'till three bubbles make
A kind of boat too fat to fit
The river. That's the end of it.

Straight
down
it
slides
and
with
a
splash

Is lost against the window sash.

Window window window pane:
Let it let it let it rain.

Write Me a Verse

I've asked Professor Swigly Brown
To talk about some kinds of Rhyme,
If you will kindly settle down.
You won't? Well, then, some other time. . . .

PROFESSOR
BROWN: The simplest of all verse to write is the couplet.
There is no argument about this: it *is* the
simplest. I have said so.

Couplet

I

A couplet is two lines — two lines in rhyme.
The first comes easy, the second may take time.

2

Most couplets will have lines of equal length;
This gives them double dignity and strength.

3

Please count the syllables in 2 and say
How many. Ten each line? Correct! And they

4

In turn comprise the five-foot standard line:
Pentameter. The foot's *iambic.* Fine

5

Enough! On human feet, of course, our shoes
Do match; likewise the laces. If you choose

6

A briefer line,
Like this of mine,

7

Or say
O.K.

8

Why, *these* are couplets, somewhat crude but true
To form. Try one yourself. See how you do.

9

Meanwhile, I'll give *you* one. Hand me that pen.
A four-foot line — eight syllables, not ten:

10

I cán / not síng / the óld / songs nów;

I név / er cóuld / sing án / y hów.

11

Couplets, you see, should make their stand alone.
I've used some differently, but that's my own

12

responsibility.

PROFESSOR
BROWN: We come now to the second easiest form of
verse: the quatrain. Since the quatrain in
length equals *two* couplets, it ought to be just
twice as easy to write. It isn't . . . it isn't.

Quatrain

1

When there is more to say — or more than planned —
A couplet's very easy to expand.
Expansive couplets, then, if out of hand,
May nicely run to four lines. Understand?

2

Four lines — quatrain; long lines or short,
But *good* lines, with a good report
Of one another as they progress.
Note one / an oth / er for change / of stress

3

Or emphasis: the sudden sharpening pace.
A quatrain says its say with perfect grace.
"I strove with none, for none was worth my strife" —
First line of four* to haunt you all your life.

4

I'll not attempt a long example —
I mean with lines of many feet;
But still you ought to have a sample
Or two to prove the form *is* neat.

* A famous quatrain by Walter Savage Landor.

5

Here goes:
Suppose
Suppose
Suppose

6

The ship sails for Spain,
For Spain the ship sails;
You can't go by train,
For a train runs on rails.

7

Let's sail a ship for far-off Spain;
We really can't get there by train.
But still a big ship has no sails;
Why not a train that has no rails?

8

Note rhymes in 1 — the rhyme control is *planned*.
In 2, *two* pairs of rhymes; in 6 we find
abab (*Spain, sails, train, rails*). Last kind
Is this (abba): *planned, find, kind, and*

9

Forget that ship that has no sails.
Let's jet by plane across to Spain
Above the sea they call the Main.
(Say something here that rhymes with *sails*.)

PROFESSOR
BROWN: The limerick, by all odds, is the most popular short verse form in English. Hundreds of people write hundreds of wretched limericks every day. Somehow they fail to understand that the limerick, to be lively and successful, *must* have *perfect* rhyming and *flawless* rhythm. The limerick form is far older than Edward Lear (1812–1888), but it was he who first made it popular. Keep it so. It needs help.

I

A limerick shapes to the eye
Like a small very squat butterfly,
　　With its wings opened wide,
　　Lots of nectar inside,
And a terrible urge to fly high.

2

The limerick's lively to write:
Five lines to it — all nice and tight.
    Two long ones, two trick
    Little short ones; then quick
As a flash here's the last one in sight.

3

Some limericks — most of them, reely —
Make ryhmes fit some key word like *Greely*
    (A man) of *Dubuque*
    (Rhymed with cucumber — cuque)
Or a Sealyham (dog). Here it's *Seely*.

4

There once was a scarecrow named Joel
Who couldn't scare crows, save his soel.
    But the crows put the scare
    Into Joel. He's not there
Any more. That's his hat on the poel.

5

"There was an old man" of wherever
You like, thus the limerick never
    Accounts for the young:
    You will find him unsung
Whether stupid, wise, foolish, or clever.

There was a young man, let me say,
Of West Pumpkinville, Maine, U.S.A.
You tell me there's not
Such a place? Thanks a lot.
I forget what he did anyway.

Take the curious case of Tom Pettigrew
And Hetty, his sister. When Hettigrew
As tall as a tree
She came just to Tom's knee.
And did *Tom* keep on growing? You bettigrew.

Consider this odd little snail
Who lives on the rim of a pail:
Often wet, never drowned,
He is always around
Safe and sound, sticking tight to his trail.

A man who was fond of his skunk
Thought he smelled pure and pungent as punk.
But his friends cried No, no,
No, no, no, no, no, *no!*
He just stinks, or he stank, or he stunk.

It's been a bad year for the moles
Who live just in stockings with holes;
    And bad for the mice
    Who prefer their boiled rice
Served in shoes that don't have any soles.

11

There once was a man on the Moon,
But he got there a little too soon.
    Some others came later
    And fell down a crater —
When *was* it? Next August? Last June?

12

"This season our tunnips was red
And them beets was all white. And instead
    Of green cabbages, what
    You suspect that we got?"
"I don't know." "Didn't plant none," he said.

13

I don't much exactly quite care
For these cats with short ears and long hair;
    But if anything's worse
    It's the very reverse:
Just you ask any mouse anywhere.

14

Write a limerick now. Say there was
An old man of some place, what he does,
    Or perhaps what he doesn't,
    Or isn't or wasn't.
Want help with it? Give me a buzz.

Jam

"Spread," said Toast to Butter,
And Butter spread.
"That's better, Butter,"
Toast said.

"Jam," said Butter to Toast.
"Where are you, Jam,
When we need you most?"
Jam: "Here I am,

Strawberry, trickly and sweet.
How are you, Spoon?"
"I'm helping somebody eat,
I think, pretty soon."

Mingram Mo

There was a man named Mingram Mo
Who never knew just where to go.
Mo had a friend — I forget his name —
Who never knew from whence he came.
And then Mo's sister, Mrs. Kriss,
Would misremember most of this,
And say to Mingram: "Mingram Mo,
What is it that you never know?
And who's this friend who knows it less?"
(His name still slips me, I confess.)
Whereat poor Mingram would invent
A place to go to when he went,
Wherein his friend called — never mind —
Might feel quite not so left behind.
But where *that* was, his sister Mrs.
Kriss still misremembers. This is
All that you will ever know of
Mingram Mo, by Jove, by Jo-of.

After Christmas

There were lots on the farm,
But the turkeys are gone.
They were gobbling alarm:
There were lots on the farm,
Did they come to some harm,
Like that poor little fawn?
There were lots on the farm,
But the turkeys are gone.

Spelling Bee

It takes a good speller
to spell *cellar*,
separate, and *benefiting*;
not omitting
cemetery, *cataclysm*,
picnicker and *pessimism*.
And have you ever tried
innocuous, *inoculate*,
dessert, *deserted*, *desiccate*;
divide and *spied*,
gnat, *knickers*, *gnome*,
crumb, *crypt*, and *chrome*;
surreptitious, *supersede*,
delete, *dilate*, *impede*?

Four Little Ducks

One little duck
In a pond is ducky:
A duck with luck.
Then lucky lucky

Two little ducks
And the pond grows duckier;
Three little ducks
And the ducks' luck luckier.

Four little ducks
Set the big geese hissing.
The old hen clucks
"Four ducks are missing!"

"Four little ducklings,"
Geese tell gander.
Curious clucklings:
Old hen *and* her

Chicks (cheep cheep)
Begin to chorus,
"Ducks! (peep peep)
In the pond before us."

The ducklings quack
Quacks high and thready:
"We won't come back
Until we're ready."

"And when will *that* be?
When? O *when?*"
"O geese O gee!
O when O hen!"

"Fresh young quackers,
Don't you think?"
"Wisecrack crackers!
Let them sink."

The geese hiss hisses,
Hen clucks clucks
With hits and misses
At those young ducks.

The ducklings quack quack
Back: "Don't meddle!"
They jibe and tack
(They really pedal);

The quacklings duck
(They're upside down);
Perhaps they're stuck,
Perhaps they'll drown;

Perhaps they'll not,
Perhaps they won't;
They know a lot.
Don't think they don't.

Four little webby
Pinkfoot truants;
It's just well mebbe
They lack influence

And don't know how
Much risk is risky.
A turtle, now,
Could snap one frisky

Foolish swimmer.
They have no mom.
Their chance grows dimmer
As they grow calm.

A turtle big
And round and flat?
The ducks don't dig
A thing like that.

A shadow glides
Up from the mud
Toward undersides
Of flesh and blood.

Old Snap's sharp eye
Has seen them pass.
The pedals fly:
They swim on glass.

Which yellow sailor
Will turtle take?
The geese grow paler,
The chicks all shake.

"Look out! Look *out!*"
The geese give warning.
But geese can't shout.
Well, just this morning,

To round them up
Is a boy out rowing.
His dog's no pup:
A wise old knowing

Red retriever,
Name of Thor,
A firm believer
In ducks ashore.

His mouth drools drooly,
Soft and quick;
He does things coolly,
Knows each trick

And duckly skitter:
All old hat
To Thor, more fitter
Than any cat.

He's poised and ready
With big-dog splash!
He's swimming steady
While ducklings dash,

Till one gets caught
And two get caughter,
As three well ought
And four well oughter.

One says, "Yes,"
The second, "Yessir!"
The pond grows less
And less and lesser

Full of flighty
Ducklings. Thor
Gives one good mighty
Shake, once more

Inside the boat.
The big drops shaken
From his red coat,
The unforsaken

Fluffy clutch
Of ducks together
Quack — as much
To say "What weather!"

Geese stop hissing,
Hen-clucks cease.
There's not one missing.
All is peace.

In pondy muck
For Snap no dinner.
No duck, no luck;
He's thin, he's thinner.

The days go by.
No duck appears.
Why magnify
My lack of tears?

Dividing

Here is an apple, ripe and red
  On one side; on the other green.
And I must cut it with a knife
  Across or in between.

And if I cut it in between,
  And give the best (as Mother said)
To you, then I must keep the green,
  And you will have the red.

But Mother says that green is tough
  Unless it comes in applesauce.
You *know* what? I've been sick enough:
  I'll cut it straight across.

The Wind

Wind in the garden,
Wind on the hill,
Wind I-am-blowing,
Never be still.

Wind I-am-blowing,
I love you the best:
Out of the morning,
Into the west.

Out of the morning,
Washed in the blue,
Wind I-am-blowing,
Where are you?

Hammock

Our hammock swings between two trees,
So when the garden's full of bees,
And if the hammock's full of me,
They fly right over, bee by bee.
They fly goshawful fast and straight —
I guess a bee is never late;
And if I can't quite see the line,
I try to think I hear the whine:
Much higher than the drowsy sound
Of having hives of bees around.
Provided bees don't bother me,
I'm glad to let a bee just be.
Some day I'll put a microphone
Inside their door and pipe the drone

Above my hammock, fall asleep
To bees all busy-buzz that keep
Their distance. Meanwhile here I lie.
I'm watching now a butterfly,
Unhurried, knowing not what's up:
A daisy, rose, or buttercup?
Not caring where he's been, or where
He's flapping to. He fills the air
With little flags and floats away
As I do on this summer's day.

This is My Rock

This is my rock,
And here I run
To steal the secret of the sun;

This is my rock,
And here come I
Before the night has swept the sky;

This is my rock,
This is the place
I meet the evening face to face.

Tomorrows

Tomorrows never seem to stay,
Tomorrow will be yesterday
Before you know.
Tomorrows have a sorry way
Of turning into just today,
And so . . . and so . . .

STARTLING VERSE FOR ALL THE FAMILY
Spike Milligan

The master of comic verse is back! Whether you're five or five hundred years old, you'll enjoy the irresistible poems that spill out of the pages of this new collection. A fun book for all the family and everyone else too.

CAT AMONG THE PIGEONS
Kit Wright

This is no ordinary collection of poems – there aren't many poetry books with singing potatoes, mad dinner ladies and zoobs in. What's a zoob? You'll have to read this book to find out!

SMILE PLEASE!
Tony Bradman

Neil has a problem with the wobbly wheel on his bike, then there's Helen who can't stop bouncing, and Sarah who can't stop skipping and Paul who likes kicking his football against the wall . . . just a few of the great people we can meet in Tony Bradman's first collection of poetry, and there's plenty of fun on every page.

THE EARTHSICK ASTRONAUT

In this original and exciting collection of children's poems, chosen from entries to *The Observer* National Poetry Competition, the earth is seen through many different eyes. Viewed from a distance by the astronaut and from the closest of quarters by the worm and the mole, our planet and its inhabitants show an infinite variety of shape and character, all drawn in vivid images by some of today's most promising poets.

OF CATERPILLARS, CATS AND CATTLE

Poems about Animals

Chosen by Anne Harvey

Dogs and frogs, cats and bats, dragonflies and butterflies . . . all these creatures and more are to be found in the poems that make up this delightful anthology selected by Anne Harvey.

Poems short and long, funny and sad, classic and modern; a very varied and enjoyable collection that will appeal to a wide range of readers.

NAILING THE SHADOW

Roger McGough

A book of poems for everyone who loves to play with words and ideas. Stylish and entertaining, this is an unbeatable new book by one of our top poets.